T0063959

WALTER PIGEON SAVES AMERICA

Richard Baron

authorHOUSE®

AuthorHouse™ LLC
1663 Liberty Drive
Bloomington, IN 47403
www.authorhouse.com
Phone: 1-800-839-8640

Published by AuthorHouse   01/14/2014

ISBN: 978-1-4918-4939-2 (sc)
ISBN: 978-1-4918-4940-8 (e)

Library of Congress Control Number: 2014900228

DEDICATION

I would like to dedicate this Book to God first and foremost, who is the Father of inspiration, Pastor John Haggie for putting the Idea of an EMP Bomb in my brain one Sunday morning, and last, WalMart INC, that is placed right down the Block from the RR bridge, where I first saw the Pigeons in route to work there.

PROLOGUE

While America folded its collective hands, and went to sleep, being concerned only about economics, entertainment, and ecology, sinister forces planned, and assembled the demise and invasion of the fatted calf formerly known as America. The Pigeon Family also slept under a rail road bridge in a small NJ town unaware of the EMP Bomb ready to explode over the entire continent rendering all electricity void, plunging the country into the 1800'ds darkness, and vaulting the once maligned Pigeon into the forefront of the battle and subsequent stardom, led by Walter.

CHAPTER 1

Humble Beginnings

Score opens up with footage from an old George Carlin concert where he talks about New York City pigeons. "Pigeons," he says, "they don't fly away from people in fright, they just walk out of your way and give you a bad look."

Fade to a New York City street-crossing with a few pigeons seemingly volleying for food in and out of the ebb and flow of traffic. A person throws out a crumb in passing and the young, tough pigeon says "Gee thanks, Sir, what would we do if it weren't for your kindness? So magnanimous of you." At the same moment, another young NYC pige takes the morsel out of the first pigeons mouth. "Hey," yelled the first pigeon, "that was *my* crumb, Dude."

The other pigeon barked over his shoulder with the crumb in his mouth, "Finders keepers, losers weepers, Dude."

"You found that in my mouth," and smacked the young pige on the back, ejecting the crumb from the thief's mouth. The thief turned around in protest and the two pigeons got into a mini tussle; meanwhile the crumb continued rolling ahead and is picked up by a larger, older pigeon who swallows it up immediately. The two boys stop fighting, shrug their shoulders and run off after other crumbs.

Fade to a neighboring New Jersey scene. Under a bridge, in a run-down industrial area, noisy traffic speeds through, water puddles everywhere and it is cold. Some pigeons are crowding together near a sunny shelf, basking to keep warm. Three of the larger, older and plumper pigeons were hogging most of the sun, eyes closed, snoring, dreaming of sweet cake crumbs raining down from the sky by the thousands, when one by one some baby birds start sneaking into sunny positions in front of the older boys for warmth. Soon there are 7 or 8 of them crowding in front of the old boys, who upon opening their eyes, are unpleasantly surprised at these nervy upstarts. The middle bird knowingly looked at the other two friends and they all broke into an evil laugh. The end bird suddenly screamed "Cat! Cat! Here comes a cat!" The little birds went into panic mode, bumping into each other as they ran off to their dens. One of the mother birds boldly came to stand before the three. "You should be ashamed of yourselves, fellas. Hogging the sun for yourselves and not sharing with the kids."

The end bird explained, "I was just dreaming of a cat, ma'am, that's all. We wouldn't do that to the kids."

"Sure you wouldn't. You're not selfish, overfed old boys, are you?" She slapped the end bird, turned away and went into the den. "Did you boys brush your beaks?"

"Yeah, Mom," a little voice answered.

The three old boys looked at each other sheepishly. "Wasn't my idea," said the middle bird, "it was yours," he said, pointing to the other bird.

"P-U!," said the other end bird holding his beak, "did you use deodorant today? You stink!"

The offending bird lifts up his wing and sniffs, his eyes cross and he falls over, unconscious.

A handsome robin with spectacles is interviewing the other birds of suburbia on the nature of pigeons. Holding a microphone in hand, he says, "this is Robbie Robin of Eyewitless News for the fly-by media. What do you think of these pigeons, Sir?," as he shoves the mic in front of two bluebirds.

"Are pigeons birds? I thought they were descendents of squirrels, but even squirrels work hard at gathering food."

"Yeah," cried a young sparrow. "They're stupid. They wouldn't know what to do with a worm if it bit them on the foot."

"Yeah," said a starling. "They're too cozy with humans. I don't trust them."

"Yeah," said a mockingbird. "They beg from humans and are looking for hand-outs all the time."

CHAPTER 2

Walter and Eddie

Two of the young pigeon friends, Walter and Eddie, who had grown up together, were the most adventuresome birds of the bunch. They would explore much further territory than their families would allow. They would say, "we're flying down the block", and take off miles away looking for adventure and would be back before anyone knew where or what they would be up to; and then mysteriously always found their way back. They both felt that they wouldn't end up under the railroad bridge like all of their friends and family. Walter in particular, thought he was destined for something bigger than the pigeon city life. He loved to fly way more than the other pigeons. They used flight as a means to get food and water or from here to there, but Walter and Eddie would fly and glide in the wind currents for hours; they never took flying for granted. They invented flying games and kept challenging and pushing each other farther and farther. They did not realize it, but they were being primed for an adventure that would be far more exciting and fulfilling than they could ever have imagined.

The two young pigeons take off together and fly to Suburbia where they are immediately harassed by the other birds there. However, they meet 'Miss Quirky Turky', who is a misplaced, lonely turkey stuck in the suburbs and she tells them about her former turkey tribe and about their storied ancestry. She directs them to a homing pigeon lodge on the top of a nearby building.

The boys flew up to the top of the main house structure to a ledge on the corner, eyes and beaks wide open. There were empty coups on one end of the open roof and then the other half of the roof was filled with exercise machines. An incredible mini gymnasium designed for birds of flight. Suddenly, they heard the deafening sound of hundreds of pigeon wings as a cloud of pigeons flew overhead in a tight formation. They rose higher and higher, and then tilted left and flew as a group every way they turned, rose or dove, never breaking rank. The boys were sorely impressed.

"Wow, Walt," choked Eddie, "these dudes are awesome!!"

"Yeah! Holy crow, Eddie," Walter replied, "these guys are what I want to be!"

The door to the roof opened and a man followed by a boy walked over to the coups. The boy saw Walter and Eddie on the far corner.

"Hey, Dad," he shouted, "take a look at these Rock pigeons."

The boy started to walk toward Walter and Eddie, but the boys freaked and bolted off the roof as fast as they could towards home.

"Hey, Pop," yelled Austin, "they're really moving for Rock pigeons," scratching his head. "Wow, look at them go!"

Walter flew back to the top of an adjacent building, followed by the puzzled Eddie.

"What are we doing here, Bro?," he asked.

"Shush!," replied Walter, "let's just wait here until the humans leave. I want to talk to the other pigeons when they land."

The formation of birds landed after a few minutes and all went over to the little gymnasium. The two humans soon went back through the door of the main house.

"Ok, Eddie, let's go check those guys out."

The young pigeons are amazed at the flying formations of their homing-pigeon brethren and fly up to their coops to initiate a dialogue. They find the homing pigeons to be self-absorbed, empty lemmings, having no idea why or what they do nor how they got there. All the homing pigeons know is that they are well-fed and in good flying shape, though they are afraid to explore anything outside their little existence.

The two boys looked around at the mini gymnasium that Austin and his dad had set up for the homing pigeons. It was very crowded with pigeons at every machine and some standing around waiting. Walter and Eddie noticed as they stood close to the other pigeons that they were a bit bigger than all of these birds. It made them feel a little superior to these birds until they noticed how strong they were as they worked out on the machines.

"Oh, I can do as many reps with this weight, too," bragged Eddie as he sat down on the machine and grabbed the handle. He started pushing his wings forward, but to his surprise, it was much harder to move his wings. "One, uh-two, whew!, three." He was obviously straining. "Ah, that's enough, it's no problem," he said, getting up from the bench.

"Yeah, sure Eddie, you can do that just like them," He said as he tilted his head and stared at Eddie in a fatherly way.

"Well, maybe these little guys are in a bit better shape than we are, but they work out all the time, right?," explained Eddie.

"Oh yeah, Eddie. How about a lot better shape," Walter sarcastically pointed out. "We got a lot of work to do, Dude, before we can be as fit as these dudes." Walter looked around and realized it was getting late. "Let's go home, Eddie-oh, I mean Super Bird."

They both laughed and were off in a flash toward home.

The two friends made a bee-line for their home under the railroad bridge, just in time for lunch. Maybe 3 or 4 times per week the fireman would come and feed the pigeons in an abandoned parking lot entrance next to the bridge. The food was good and the whole tribe looked forward to and counted on these feeding extravaganzas or frenzies, because that's what they were. It was mostly pigeons who were present. No other birds really came down to this area very often and it was safe. No cats would come by when there was a human present, as they did at other times, looking for a stray pigeon or two. Every once in a great while they were successful, which caused great anxiety in the pigeon community. But for now, it was a free-for-all buffet of bread, seed, nuts and crackers.

"OH, YEAH!!"

After the great lunch, the boys sought of their Grandpa and a few of the other older pigeons. Because of these mass feedings of the last few years, the old boys were quite plump. Less flying and more feeding led to some hefty old boys. Walter and Eddie found the oldsters sitting on their usual ledge, sunning themselves, half falling asleep.

Walter sheepishly approached the so-oozy pack of plump pigeons, "Uh, ahem, Grandpa?" He didn't get any response, so he tried again, but a bit louder, "Uh, Grandpa?"

The pack startled as one big wave, then looked at the two youths menacingly. Grandpa retorted sternly, "Boy, can't you see we're busy? Come back later."

"But Grandpa, me and Eddie need to talk to you now," he insisted.

"Well, what is it, boys, this better be good," Grandpa replied with his eyebrows furrowed.

"Well," Walter answered, "me and Eddie discovered a homing pigeon coup."

Every one of the old men snapped out of their sleepy stupor immediately.

"What were you doing so far from home?," Grandpa quizzed.

Walter answered with a question, "You know of these other pigeons? Why didn't you tell us about them?"

Grandpa answered defensively, "Well, who cares about them? Just be concerned with your own tribe, boy!"

Walter got mad at his Grandpa for the first time. "Grandpa! I want to know! We want to know what you know about these and all pigeons. We heard from a turkey that we were not always beggars."

Grandpa looked sheepishly at the other old boys who were trying to tell him not to divulge their well-kept secret. He finally sighed, "Ok, ok, but don't go blabbing this to the others, promise?"

"All right, Grandpa. We promise," he replied.

Grandpa began, "Well boys, my Grandpa told me that his Grandpa said us pigeons were a very important, prestigious and goal-oriented bird. We flew great distances under enormous pressure, without ever getting lost." He went on proudly, "Mankind harnessed this gift from the maker, to use us as couriers during peacetime and wartime. This use of pigeons goes back to almost the beginning of time. We can't imagine how far back, but man keeps track of time, he knows. Why, I heard that in ancient times there was a world-wide flood and our cousins the doves were used to find dry land.

"Now in recent times, because of man's inventions, we are no longer deemed necessary for communication. People now talk to each other through the black wires we perch on every day, and now through the air. Haven't you two ever heard the voices of men and music coming out of the boxes or cages they move around in?"

"Yeah," they both replied, wide-eyed and beaks open; it now all made sense.

Grandpa looked down, but continued, "Now for quite some time we've become irrelevant, so we scavenge and beg for a living."

Eddie chimed in, "But what about the homing pigeons?"

"Well," Grandpa answered, "man uses some of us as a hobby, to amuse himself. He loves to play games, don't you know. But those birds aren't as free as we are." Now Grandpa looked angry once again and asked, "Now what were you two doing so far from home?"

Walter replied proudly, "We don't consider that very far at all, Grandpa."

Eddie added without thinking, "Yeah, sure, we go way farther than that." Realizing he misspoke, he nervously turned to Walter.

Grandpa and the others scowled back angrily, "Way farther?," he snorted.

"Yes, Grandpa," he fired back defiantly, "we're not babies any longer, you know, and unlike most of you who go from here to Walmart to beg for food, we love to explore and fly and use the gift the Maker gave us."

"But you're in great danger out there, son," he replied pleadingly, realizing the two weren't accountable to him any longer.

"Grandpa, remember Benny?," Walter sadly asked. "A cat got him right here in the parking lot because he wasn't paying attention. Me and Eddie got each other's back, we're constantly looking out for danger. And even if something bad were to happen to either of us at least we went being happy and free and flying which we love to do most of all. You should be happy and proud for us, Gramps," he finished.

Grandpa's eyes softened and a smile crossed his beak, "Ok, Ok, boys. We realize you're old enough, and yes, we're always bragging about you, but we worry because we love you," he explained, wrapping his wings around Walter. "Now get out of here, you worm heads, we never had this conversation, right?"

"Thanks, Grandpa," they nodded in agreement, "see you all tonight."

CHAPTER 3

Mumford, the Translator

Walter was ready to take off for the pigeon coup when his eye caught an unusually bright color on the telephone wire some 50 feet east of the railroad bridge.

"What the heck?," exclaimed Walter. "What is that on the wire, Eddie?"

"Looks like a bird or something," he guessed. But before he could say another word, Walter was off in a shot, landing next to the bright colored thing on the wire. It was a bird after all, a blue-fronted Amazon, mostly green in color, with a bluish front and yellow rings around his eyes. The two birds immediately sized each other up; they seemed to be the same size. Eddie then landed on the other side of the strange green bird, causing him to look nervously from Walter to Eddie and back.

"Hey guys, wha-what's going on? I'm feeling like a chicken salad sandwich here. I warn you, I know karate and am lethal with both wings, ambiwingstress."

Walter answered in a friendly tone, "Hi, dude. I'm Walter and this is my best buddy, Eddie."

Eddie saluted. "What kind of bird are you, dude?"

The 'deadly' green bird fluffed his feathers in relief and relaxed a bit. "I'm Mumford, a parrot. What. You never saw a parrot?"

"No," replied Walter, "we never saw a bird like you before. Where do you come from, dude?"

"Well," explained Mumford, "my tribe is from the tropics, way far south of this land. I, unfortunately, was born in a pet shop and been caged up most of my life. I just escaped from a house in town where the people were treating me very badly. The dummies left the kitchen window open and when they opened the cage to change my water, I bolted."

"Why didn't you like the people?," Walter asked.

"Well," he answered sarcastically, "I do like to eat and drink regularly, don't you?"

"Yeah, of course we do," said Walter.

Mumford added, "not only that, but for no particular reason they would throw stuff at my cage, to scare the living poop out of me." He went on, "the house was always cold, man, and I hate the cold. And furthermore, they cursed like sailors. I learned some heavt-duty curse words, dudes, and when they did bad stuff to me, I let them have it, both barrels. Then they threatened to choke the life out of me. So I just shut my beak and waited for my chance to escape."

Walter's eyes were wide open with excitement. "Dude, you got guts!"

"Yeah, we like guts," Eddie said.

"Hey, Mumford," Walter said, "want to hang with us? We don't curse."

"Well, yeah, of course. It's not like I have my social calendar all booked up, Walter. But I'll tell you boys, I'm starving. Do you think anyone would mind if I flew down and partook in the smorgasbord over yonder?," he asked, pointing to the pigeons feeding below.

"Yeah, Mumph, follow us down, come on," Walter said, waving his wing.

The three flew down to the driveway, littered with leftover scraps.

Eddie spoke, "We'll keep watch out for cats, Mumph, you just eat, pal."

They really liked this lonely little parrot who seemed to eat for the longest time. Walter couldn't believe his appetite.

"Boy, you can pack it away for a skinny guy, heh."

Later, when they were sitting around talking, Walter asked, "Hey, Mumph, you said you cursed at the people? You actually talked to them and they understood you?"

Mumford cleared his throat, "Well yeah, I just don't mimic them, I can have a conversation with them."

A light went on in Walter's little brain.

"Could you do me a BIG favor, Mumph? Ol' buddy, ol' pal."

"Sure, Walt, I'll do anything for you, give you up to half my kingdom."

Walter continued, "I need you to talk to a couple of men for me, the ones who run the pigeon coup in town. Me and Eddie want to join, and with your help we can do it."

Mumford smirked, "Why would you want to do that? Seems to me you have a good life right here."

"Good, yes, but boring. We feel we were destined for greater things," Walter said.

"Yeah," Eddie chimed in proudly.

"Wow," Mumford said sadly, "I just met you guys and you want to join the Air Force?"

"Sorry, Mumph," Walter added apologetically, "but yes, we do. Come with us and join the coup, be the translator, be our helper," he pleaded.

"Ok," Mumford resigned, "let's do it. Show me where the place is."

The three of them(Walter, Eddie and Mumford) strike out for the pigeon coop. They arrive there to find a young boy about 8 years old, named Austin, sitting on a milk crate talking to himself and the pigeons he is feeding. The three birds land on the roof ledge near the coop and Austin. Austin stops what he's doing and talks to the group, "Hey guys, what are you doing up here? And wow, a beautiful parrot! What are you doing with these pigeons?"

"Hello, young dude, how are you doing?," Mumford asked.

Austin's eyes flew open wide as he dropped the feeding shovel on the floor of the roof. "You talked to me!," exclaimed Austin. "What the-"

"Sure," retorted Mumford, "I talk to everybody. My name is Mumford and these are my friends Walter and Eddie. What's your name?"

"Austin," he said smiling, "what are you guys doing way up here?"

"Well," said Mumford, "we've come to see if you can help my friends fulfill a dream of theirs."

"Me? A dream? What?"

"Walter and Eddie would like to become homing or carrier pigeons."

"What?!," exclaimed Austin, who then broke out into a hearty laugh that almost lasted a bit too long, Austin recovers himself to explain that homing pigeons are born, bred and trained and points out to the three birds some of the pigeons in the coop who excel in their flying skills. Each one seems to be very prideful. Mumford angrily turns toward his two friends to ask them about what they thought. Walter indignantly tells him about some of his flying prowess and close calls. He challenges any of the other pigeons to a flying duel. Mumford explains to Austin what Walter has said.

CHAPTER 4

Joining the Coup

"Really?," Austin said, stroking his chin. "Hmm, very interesting. Ya know, it gets pretty boring up here most days. This could really be cool, let me think." He continued stroking his chin while looking over the three birds. "Ok, I have a great idea. Let's have a race between Walter, Eddie and my two champions! I will let my two out for their normal run of three laps with some difficult turns. Let's see if Walter and Eddie can keep up and follow closely."

Austin gets his two arrogant champions out of their coop and lines them all up and gives them their pre-flight instructions. He yells "Go!" as he raises his arms and the birds are off!

The four take off, making a large right circle then turn upward as they go. Surprisingly, Walter and Eddie, the slightly larger of the four birds, are keeping up with the two champions. Suddenly, the two champs turn left on a dime, catching Walter and Eddie off-guard. As a result, their turn is much wider, but they quickly adjust and close the gap. Now diving down quickly, turning right and starting back up again then left toward the coop, passing in a flash. 1st lap completed! Now the birds run the 2nd lap identically, this time our two friends keeping up with the turns but staring to tire toward the end of the lap. The route of the race, being ingrained into the two champions minds, their 3rd lap's turns, dives and climbs came instinctively. Although Walter and Eddie had begun to learn the pattern of the race, they were falling behind badly. Due to the lack of training, when they reached the apex of the course, all hope of keeping up with the champs seemed lost. Walter said to Eddie, "follow my lead, no matter what happens" and he dove straight down, cutting the course in half. At the bottom he turned, back on course, entering just ahead of the champs. In a burst of energy, Walter came to land on the top of the pigeon coop, followed hotly by the two champs, then Eddie.

"Hey!," yelled Austin, "that's cheating! I saw that move! My two champions are still champs! They don't realize what you've just done." Austin stopped short and a puzzled look came over his face. "Wait a minute, just who are you, little Walter? That was a brilliant move! Way too over the top for a little brain like yours."

Walter walked over to Mumford and excitedly cooed and cooed, flapping his wings emotionally. Mumford then sidled over to Austin. "You see young chap, Walter realizes that he and Eddie are out of shape. He hates losing so much and he wanted to show you he has other qualities, like thinking outside the box to get the job done. He says he's sorry, but he needed to get your attention so that you'd let him and Eddie into your homing pigeon coop. He says with a little training he'd be able to keep up with most of your birds. He's not too sure about your champions, though he does think they are awesome."

Austin's face softened and his body relaxed. "Wow, you guys really want to join the coop? Well, I'll have to give it some thought and I'll have to ask my father, 'cause he's the real boss around here."

At first, the father doesn't like the idea of new birds coming into the closed community, and street birds at that. But Austin told his father about the uniqueness of one little bird named Walter and finally, the father agrees to try them out for a short period, since Austin felt really strongly. Austin was a very hard-working boy and had the respect of his father. The training begins.

"Ok," Austin says, "you guys are in!" Followed by much jubilation and high-fives. "Now listen, first thing is you must go home and tell your family what you'll be doing. You'll be away for some time, this will be a big commitment. So say your 'good-byes' and come back as soon as you can."

So the three birds fly off to their homes under the bridge to bid their families a tearful farewell. They report back to Austin's coop the following day. Mumford states that he will go along as 'advisor & observer'. "That's what I am," he says.

Austin takes the three birds to a wooden door directly in the back of the exposed coop, puts his hands on the lever and says, "Well gentlemen, any one not sure he wants to be here or have any thoughts about this next phase of training?"

Walter and Eddie look sheepishly at each other and then back to Austin, "Nope, we're psyched! Let's go, dude!"

"Ok," Austin replies sarcastically, "welcome to Boot Camp, little dudes!" He clicks the lever and they go into a training gym.

This larger portion of the flat roof was an immense gymnasium littered with little weight benches, elliptical machines and treadmills. There were about 40 pigeons working out on various machines, but standing in front of them were two very formidable pigeons, Colonel Roberts and Sergeant Vega.

"Walter, Eddie, I now put you into the capable hands of Col. Roberts and Sgt Vega." Austin saluted the two army birds and said, "Take good care of these two and report back to me," he ordered.

"Yes, Sir!," the two army birds retorted in unison as they returned Austin's salute.

Mumford jumped in and started to explain his position in all this, but Col. Roberts abruptly stopped him and started to shout in military fashion, "Ok you beefed-up birds, you're mine for the next 4 weeks!" He continued to address the two friends and point out their obvious defects. "Stick out your chest! Beaks forward! Stomach in, feet straight ahead!"

Looking into Walter and Eddie's eyes beak-to-beak, Sgt Vega asked sarcastically, "So you want to join our force, be a carrier, huh? Did you ask your mommies if you could join?" The boys wisely stayed quiet and stared straight ahead of them. "You softies are going to wish you never came through this door. I'll bet you go running home to your mommies, right Colonel?"

The boys noticed a huge cone-shaped cylinder on large wheels sitting horizontally but slightly tilted toward the sky like a great big lampshade.

Roberts and Vega brought the boys directly in front of the opening of the great machine.

"Ok you two, when I throw this switch, start flying into the wind and we'll see how far you need to go," Vega said. "Ready . . . set . . . GO!," he yelled as he threw the switch. A blast of air threw the boys back on their butts and against a brick wall, but they quickly got up and started flying into the wind. They started to make slow progress toward the cone when Vega laughed and pressed another switch which increased the force by one-quarter. The boys' progress had been stopped and now they were being driven back toward the wall. The two flapped their wings mightily and began to inch forward again toward the giant cone.

"Come on, girls!," the Colonel boomed, "you've gotta move faster than that! How are you gonna keep up with my flock? What a sorry excuse for flying you are!"

He then threw a larger switch all the way forward and the machine blew with a fierce velocity full speed. It blew the hapless birds against the wall and they fell on top of each other, panting and groaning.

"You boys have a lot of training to do! I suggest we get started right away!"

Sgt Vega took the boys over to the exercise area where a very beautiful, young, obviously fit and trim, girl pigeon stood waiting by the machines.

"Girls," he said, "this is your exercise instructor Lucy. Lucy," he instructed, "my condolences on working to get these two in shape. Do the best you can."

"Yes, sir, don't worry, they'll do just fine," she replied.

"Huh, so you say. Good luck!" He started laughing sarcastically as he walked away.

Walter just had the dumbest look on his face caused by this stunning beauty. He had never seen such a beautiful creature in all his life; he was officially love-struck. He had a hard time paying attention to the detailed instructions she rattled off and he got confused and tangled up in some of the machines. She approached him, "Walter, you seem to need some help. Didn't you pay attention to my instructions?," she asked.

"No, uh, I mean yes," he said sheepishly. "Sorry, I'm not so good with machines," he explained.

"Well," she replied, "that's why I'm here. Watch me use each machine and then try them yourself. Your buddy Eddie seems to have a knack for this."

So they worked all afternoon on the machines and it was time for dinner.

At dinner, Walter tried to get as close as possible to Lucy without tipping his hand, but she kind of got the idea that he liked her and she didn't mind as all. He made her heart skip a few beats, too, though she tried to deny it to herself. Day after day they worked out together and started to look forward to seeing each other.

Now we fast flap-forward over the next month of intense training —exercise machines—wind tunnel flying—actual flying with the flock. Spring wandered into Summer and the boys were sweating into shape. Little by little progress was steady and the Colonel and the Sgt noted the progress of the two friends. They also got quite a kick out of Mumford. They really didn't like parrots before they met him. Not bad for a slow-flying civilian-minded bird.

Mumford however, was having the time of his life, free from his abusive keepers and just the life of the party and could actually talk to people he felt comfortable with, especially Austin.

CHAPTER 5

Mumford meets the General

One day while Mumford, who was the official gofer for the boys, flew by an electronics shop and for the first time saw some large televisions showing exotic parrots from around the world. He was mesmerized by the beautiful girls from all over the world. He was perched on the back of a bench and did not notice two dark-souled youths slowly approaching him with a net and a large cloth bag. The next thing he knew, he was netted and thrown into total blackness. "What a dope," he thought. "Now what? There goes my free life!"

"Yeah!," the two boys yelled in unison excitedly. "We got this little dude, now let's go collect our money." They ran down the street excitedly toward the local pet store.

As they burst through the door, the bell rang out chaotically and Willie, the owner, who was trying to catch some tropical fish, wheeled around with an annoying look. When he saw the boys he seemed to get more aggravated; he was a little man who looked like Woody Allen in his youthful days. The boys approached him quickly. "Dude, we got the cool fancy bird that you said you'd pay handsome for."

"Oh, really" Willie said sarcastically, drumming his fingers on the top of the fish tank. "Let's see."

The boy carrying the bag slowly put his hand in the bag, slowly searching for Mumford, only to yell out loud in pain as Mumford took a nice bite out of his searching fingers. The boy then lunged in with his other hand and grabbed Mumford and dragged him out of the darkness.

The look on Willie's face changed abruptly from disgust to wonder. "Where did you get this bird?" He made it very obvious he was interested.

"Dude, he was down in front of the TV shop watching some bird show on Animal Planet."

"Hey! Take your hands off me!," Mumford screamed, making them stop and stare in shock.

"And he talks, too!," Willie exclaimed. "Let me see this creature." He gently took Mumford out of the hands of the boy.

"Hey, wait a minute! Ya owe us 20 bucks for this bird, dude," the bitten boy said.

"It should be more than 20, because he can talk!," the other boy piped in.

"Fine, I'll give you 30 dollars and not a penny more," Willie said shrewdly.

"We want 40, dude, or we take him and go somewhere else," the first boy said defiantly, reaching over the counter for Mumford.

"Ok, ok," Willie replied, recoiling and gripping the bird a little tighter. If any of them had been listening, they could've heard a distinct grunt come from Mumford as he was squeezed tightly. [This could be used to comic effect, if desired at this point.] "40 it is, but it's highway robbery! You're lucky I like this bird." Willie brought Mumford over to a large green, dome-shaped cage and released Mumford onto a wooden perch.

Mumford fluffed his feathers violently and was very disgusted with himself. He was beside himself that he wasn't paying attention to these crass people. "Oh, boy," he thought to himself, "back in a cage again. I can't believe I didn't see those two losers sneaking up on me."

Willie went over to his cash register and pounded the keys to give the impression to the two boys that he was upset that they were swindling him out of a lot of money, but he knew his new caged parrot was easily worth much much more. "Here's your money, boys," he said, throwing the bills on the counter, "just remember who treats you good." As the boys reached for the two 20-dollar bills gleefully, Willie slapped his hand on the bills, much to their annoyance and said, "remember to keep your eyes peeled for unattended animals, regardless if they have tags or not. I have an un-filled order in for a black Persian cat. See what you can do."

"Sure thing, Willie," the first boy said as they both snapped up their respective 20-dollar bills. They were out the door in a flash.

Willie sauntered over to the large green cage and peered intently in on Mumford. "Well, little guy, you're going to make me the money to pay the rent this month," he told the bird. "I think I could easily get $800 for you," he said, grinning slyly.

Meanwhile, back at the rooftop pigeon home, Walter and Eddie perched on the ledge of the roof staring down the avenue wondering where their animated little friend had disappeared to.

"Something's wrong, real wrong. I've got a bad feeling our little buddy is in some kind of trouble," offered Eddie with a concerned look on his face.

"I think you're right, Eddie. He's never been gone for more than an hour or so. He's such a doofus, not used to being out on the street. I think someone's got him, and if I'm right, we may never see him again."

They were startled when a voice boomed from behind them, "What are you two doing out past curfew?!"

The two wheeled around, almost losing their balance, "Uh, sorry, Sir," Walter said to Vega who had a very stern look on his face. "Mumford never came back from an errand run we sent him on over 5 hours ago. We're worried."

The harsh look softened somewhat, "the little guy is gone? That's too bad, but you two must get some sleep for tomorrow's race," Vega said, composing himself once again.

"Well, Sir, we were thinking of flying down the avenue a couple times to see if Mumford is not hurt or something. We won't be gone long," Walter said pleadingly.

"Breaking training regulations is out of the question, boys. But I'm going to make like we never had this conversation and turn in for the night. I'll give you 20 minutes to get back in your bunks or I'll turn you in. Is that clear?"

"Yes, Sir!," the boys said in unison while tending crisp salutes admiringly to Vega.

They were off in a flash. At first they didn't notice how effortless their flying was as swooped down the avenue. They slowed and eventually landed on some telephone wires and looked intently in every direction, every nook and cranny.

"Hey," Eddie said, "did you notice anything?"

"What?"

"We're not out of breath!," Eddie exclaimed.

"You know, you're right. I'm not even sweating."

"I guess the training is working."

"Look, let's just focus on looking for Mumford, we don't have much time," Walter instructed.

A half-hour later, the two young pigeons landed back on the ledge of their new home away from home. Waiting patiently, [chomping on the stub of a cigar?], was Sgt Vega. "Your 10 minutes late. I was about to turn you in."

The two said nothing. They just stood in front of their sergeant looking very dejected.

"What? You couldn't find the little guy?"

"No, Sir," Walter said. "We need to get some sleep now."

Young Austin checked in on the birds first thing in the morning and right after school. He was impressed with the progress of the two rock pigeons. He cheered them on, taking them out of training each night to talk to them even though they couldn't answer back. Tonight was no different. "Yeah, I know you guys miss Mumford, too. He is such a cool bird, but he's the kind of bird who always lands on his feet my friends and I have been looking for the little guy, but he just seemed to vanish." Then he smiled and said, "but I get a strange feeling we're all going to see him soon. Good night, boys," he said as he put them back in the training pen.

Early the next morning. Walter and Eddie were abruptly awakened by the blast of a trumpet. Everyone quickly hurried into their pre-designated groups to start this very important day. Flying formations and races were to be the highlights of the day and there would also be some humans hanging around.

This would be the first time the boys would be flying in formation with others and were to be expected to keep their turns tight as well as keeping up with the other birds. The one-month's training had produced a marvelous result in the two friends. They did everything they were asked to do, flawlessly. The Colonel and Vega were very pleased indeed, but they weren't going to let the boys know how they felt.

"Well, we've seen a little progress, but you boys have a long way to go. Keep up the hard work and you just may be good enough," the Colonel said.

The boys looked at each other, puzzled, but said, "thank you, Sir."

The boys walked off for the first break of the day. Eddie turned to Walter and said, "Gee, I thought we've been doing better than just 'OK'. What do you think?"

"Yeah, I agree. We've kept up with them all this time. All the tight turns, loops and just flat-out all the way fast flying. We held our own, Eddie," he said as he held his wing hand out for a high-five, quickly obliged by a smiling Eddie.

Their euphoria was short-lived by a loud blast of trumpets that signaled the beginning of the races.

The races were held each year during the warm season and they featured the best flyers in the squadron in head-to-head racing competitions. The boys were not allowed to join this particular season. Though they might have been improving in regards to the normal run of the pack, they clearly were no match for their championship-bred buddies. So they sat on the sidelines and watched the competition with all the other birds. The more he watched, the more Walter firmly believed that he, as well as Eddie, could compete and even win. For the first time he felt that he was special, unique, and certainly as good or better a flyer than most, if not all of these other birds. Little did he know that his time was fast approaching.

Many days had passed since Mumford was abducted and the boys were nearing the end of their training. They were so busy and tired that they had little time to lament their friend. They just hoped that he somehow landed on his feet and was doing well.

Not far from the pigeon coop at that little pet shop on the avenue, Mumford perched, fast asleep in the large green cage. He was dreaming and it was a wonderful dream. He was flying with his two friends and they were just about to hit a wall.

"AAHHH!!," he screamed, throwing open his eyes. At first he didn't know where he was, but then it hit him. He fluffed his feathers and looked disgustedly around. "Oh, joy. Back in this god-forsaken joint. Will this nightmare ever end?" He sighed tiredly.

Just then, the bell over the door clanged louder than usual and Mumford turned his head to see what was coming through the door. A dark shadow blocked out the sun from the door, it clanged shut and the huge figure strode straight toward the green cage. This guy looked like a parrot man, he was so different, so colorful, it looked like he had wings on his shoulders. He stood right in front of Mumford, cleared his throat, turned slightly and said, "is this the parrot you called me about? Hmm." He turned fully toward Mumford, "nice colors, though a bit scrawny. Say little fella, want to join the Army?"

"Yeah, like I really have a choice, dude," Mumford thought to himself. "Just take me out of here, please!"

The General cleared his throat, turned away from the cage and addressed Willie. "I think you're asking too much for this bird. I was hoping he was a bit bigger and somewhat more active."

"Oh no," Mumford thought, "I better act quick or I'll go to some old lady or a Chinaman. I don't talk Chinese." Mumford began to move back-and-forth excitedly along the perch and said aloud, "I like Ike. Attention! Hut-two-three-four, hut-two-three-four!"

The General's mouth dropped in amazement. "You didn't say this guy could talk."

"Oh, yes. That's why I am asking so much," Willie replied, running over to the cage.

"What's his name?"

"Um, I don't know," Willie said embarrassingly, "I just call him 'Polly'".

Mumford flapped excitedly, "Mumford wants a cracker." He moved back-and-forth once again, all while repeating his request for a cracker.

"Look," the General said, "he knows his name. Say, can this little guy understand what I just asked?"

"No, no, no," Willie said. "They can't converse like we can. He's just must be impressed with you. I think he likes you, Sir, he's never acted like this before with anyone else."

"Yeah? Well, I think I like this little guy, too. I'll take him."

"Very good, General. Do you have a cage for him or will you need to buy one?," he asked manipulatively.

"Yes, I'll take this green one. It's included in the price you're charging, isn't that correct?"

"Oh, no, Sir. This is a very expensive cage."

"Look, Willie, you came by Mumford in a nefarious way. So I won't press you any further if you throw in the cage. Do you understand?"

Without saying much other than a few unhappy grunts, Willie sold Mumford and the cage to the General. Moments later, they were out the door.

So now Mumford was an Army bird, just like his two long-lost buddies. How ironic, how cool, he missed them.

The General's car went through the gates of the military base to the office of the General. Mumford's cage was placed at a window near the general's large desk.

Over the next few weeks, the General and Mumford got very well-acquainted. Mumford would parrot back any phrase the General would come up with. The General then put Mumford up on his shoulder or on his desk. Mumford loved the freedom. He was very well-treated and liked the General. The food was good bird food, though the General sometimes liberally shared human food with him.

There was also a cast of characters that came through the office on a daily basis and they all groveled before the General. He had a way of making people nervous, but he would act like a child when talking to Mumford. And Mumford couldn't wait to tell his friends about this interesting Army life and this cool General that treated him like a prince and fed him food that he had never eaten before and in such large quantities! It was obvious that he had already put on some ounces.

CHAPTER 6

You're in the Army Now

Walter and Eddie had finished their basic training and flew home to see their families. They glided over the long industrial road to the railroad bridge that housed many pigeon families. Walter noticed the red fire can, which meant that the pigeons were getting their weekly feeding by the Fire Captain. Lots of bread, seeds and nuts were mixed together and spread onto the ground at the roadside, where the pigeons mobbed the feeding area in a frenzy[possibly show here why they feed in a frenzy even though they are fed weekly? Possible interaction with antagonistic seagulls which are just "passing through"?]. Pigeons had become scavengers and beggars. They weren't really good hunters or foragers; they would rather fly down to the end of the road to the local Walmart and look for scraps and hand-outs, competing for crumbs with seagulls and the occasional raven. Seagulls were the worst; loud cackling bullies. Pigeons were no match for them on the ground, but the gulls were slow flyers, almost gliders. And they were stupid as well, sometimes thinking rocks were food.

The two boys glided to a rest on the large telephone wire that ran under the bridge, paralleling the road. They watched the assortment of birds bum-rushing the food on the ground. They looked at each other knowingly and shook their heads in amazement.

"Did we do *this*?," asked Eddie.

"I guess we did," Walter replied sadly, "but it seems so long ago."

"Are you even hungry?"

"No," said Walter. "I used to be the first to enter this place, but now we feed regularly and I love it."

The two patiently sat on the wire and waited for the food to be gone. Soon they swooped down and landed near their families.

"What's up, everybody?," asked Walter.

The whole crowd stopped what they were doing upon hearing the familiar voice and stood quietly and stared in awe of these two familiar figures. Were these two really their boys? They looked familiar, but something was really different about them. They stood straighter, taller, more defined and more confident.

Many of the birds exclaimed, "Eddie! Walter!," and rushed the two boys, showering them with wings and beaks. Their mothers and fathers rubbed up against the boys in sheer delight; they must have spent an hour with the crowd asking and answering questions and telling everyone about life in the pigeon coop.

"We're so proud of you," Walter's father said smiling.

Darkness was coming, so the boys went to their individual home openings under the bridge with their families, being separated from each other's company for the first time in many weeks.

There was an inordinate amount of cooing and talking under the bridge that night. It was a wonder anyone was able to get some sleep. But one-by-one they all drifted off to dreamland, happy about their two boys coming back home. But this would be their last normal night for a long, long time.

It was very early next morning when in the still darkness a muffled THUD could be heard in the sky or somewhere off in the distance. The pigeons turned their heads and fluffed their feathers, but none fully woke. It became eerily quiet and even darker than before.

About 5 a.m. the pigeons were usually awakened by the passing of trucks coming down the road to Walmart and the Postal Depot, but this morning, none came or went. A very faint band of light was starting to appear East over New York City, but all was quiet. Too quiet.

The two boys, because of their training, were early risers, way before anyone else.

"Something's wrong," Walter said with a concerned look on his face. "It's too quiet and there's no lights anywhere. No cars or trucks. Nothing."

But there was some movement from the end of the street. People were walking in great numbers from the two large structures at the end of the road coming right towards the old railroad bridge where all the pigeons lived.

"Wow, there are hundreds of them!," Eddie said.

"This has never happened before," Walter added. "Something's up and I don't think it's good."

The people went by quickly and mostly quietly. By now, most all of the other birds had awakened and all were sitting on ledges and wires looking down at the throng of humanity walk by them.

"Listen everyone, me and Eddie are going to fly into town to see what's going on. We'll be back soon, then we must return to the coop."

So the boys flew straight into town. They flew over the main avenue gliding in circles to get a glimpse of the going's-on in the street. None of the lights above the streets were on, nor were there colored lights at the cross streets. There was no traffic and all the big metal boxes the humans traveled in sat motionless along the roadside. But all the people were out in the street in great numbers.

"Let's go down over by that large building. The wires are close enough to where all the people are gathering," Walter said.

So the boys took a quick flight and landed on the wires that ran next to the town Courthouse. Walter listened in. Miraculously, he was able to understand the human speech, he just was not able to speak it, like Mumford could. There was much commotion, but they were all talking about one topic: They were attacked by something high in the sky; a bomb, something called an 'EMP' bomb that knocked out all the electricity. That's why there were no lights or moving vehicles or anything electrical in operation. And Walter realized there was no music, something to which he loved listening to. The people seemed very afraid. The fastest things to move along the ground were bicycles and skateboards.

The boys looked at each other and without a word took off to fly home. There, they said their "good-bye's" and flew straight back to the coop.

As they landed on the top of the roof they noticed all the activity going on. Pigeons were coming and going in a frenzied pace, some marching, some flying and Austin and his Dad were there moving around excitedly, waving their hands and shouting orders. Austin looked back at the two boys, "Well, where the hell[? For an 8-year old] have you two been?! Get over here pronto!" He stuck a whistle in his mouth and blew loudly. Everyone stopped. Austin's Dad shouted, "ok, birds, listen up. We've got trouble, big trouble. Line up in your assigned ranks and listen to what's going on."

"You birds have been training and going to tournaments against other coops for as long as you can remember," Austin began. "Well, we are now about to step into a routine that only your ancestors experienced long, long ago. You are going to use all your training and flying expertise in a life and death situation to take messages between command posts for the United States Army. You see, this wonderful land we live in has been attacked by a bomb that knocked out the power that enabled humans to travel and communicate. Now pigeons will be the fastest way to speak with each other over long distances. You boys will be taken by horse and wagon some distance from here, released, to fly back to the coop. If successful, you will be given missions all over the country by the Army."

Early the next morning the pigeons were carried down from the coop and loaded onto a horse-laden wagon and off they went through the quiet streets. The horses were excited and almost gleeful as they went down city streets, unopposed to the local traffic. They were making good time to a southern point somewhere near Maryland. At dusk they arrived at what appeared to be an army base. Austin and his Dad, accompanied by several soldiers, unloaded the pigeons into a makeshift cage on the roof of a one-story building. A Major had tags put on the feet of the pigeons and a rolled-up waterproof paper was tied around each pigeons legs; a simulated message to be delivered back to the original coop.

Austin spoke briefly to Colonel Roberts and Sergeant Vega, who, in turn, addressed the other birds. "Ok, you birds," Colonel Roberts began, "listen up. Today you are going to fly farther than ever before. We're about 300 miles from our home and you are going to make this journey as fast as you can. We can do this, guys! Our ancestors would be proud of what we're about to do!"

Sgt Vega barked at the crowd, "Get in formation, now, on the double!"

The pigeons hurriedly scrambled into formation in short order. Most of the pigeons had worried looks on their faces; they've never been but a few blocks from their home and, to put it bluntly, they were scared. But our two Rock pigeons were pumped and excited. They were used to being away from their home for a few days at a time. This was going to be a cool, new adventure.

The Colonel and Sgt Vega took off, followed by the rest of the formation. Walter and Eddie brought up the rear. They flew in one wide circle then instinctively headed north. They tried a few different altitudes until they found a stream of air that was heading their way and flying became much easier. After two hours of constant flying, they were headed into black foreboding clouds full of wind, rain, and worst of all, lightning. The wind and rain became harder and harder to navigate. Walter caught up to Colonel Roberts and flew along side momentarily before speaking, "Sir," he shouted, "we should look for a bridge or some large shelter. I've flown through storms like this before and there's no winning!"

"I think you're right, son. Lead the way!"

"We'll go nearer the city, just up ahead. Something will come up."

As they approached the outskirts of the city, Walter spotted a large highway overpass and motioned to the others to follow him down. The 77 birds were swallowed up by the roadway underpass. They first gathered by the sidewalk, then flew to the ledges that lined the underside of the bridge. Moments later the rain came down in torrents as the wind and lightning raged.

There were some local Rock pigeons at the other end of the overpass, watching the motley group very curiously. The Colonel looked over at Walter and said, "good job, son." For the first time, the Colonel was glad that he let these two boys in the coop. Their enthusiasm was infectious to the other birds.

After the storm passed, the birds resumed their flight to the northeast. They found the air stream to the north and rode it to their hometown and landed on their familiar rooftop. Austin's Dad and some very important Army officers were waiting for their arrival.

After some time feeding and relaxation on their perches, the birds were summoned to the rooftop training ground where they all lined up for a briefing by Colonel Roberts. "Listen up! This land we live in is under attack by another land. We pigeons are needed by the humans to carry very important messages. The humans are counting on us very much, so we cannot let them down." He looked over the bunch carefully and shouted, "Are you ready, Pigeons?!"

"Yes, Sir!," they shouted.

"I can't hear you!!"

"YES, SIR!!," they boomed in unison.

"Move out!"

The troop was separated into 6 groups of 13 birds each. The groups would be sent to various locations around the country and would fly messages back to the coop, which had now been turned into an Army outpost, manned by Army officers to coordinate the message traffic.

Unfortunately, Walter and Eddie were assigned into different groups. In Colonel Roberts mind, he needed strong leaders to head each group and the two boys needed to be in separate groups. He knew these two friends were not afraid of new settings.

The United States was attacked by another country who had been planning the attack and subsequent invasion for many years. First, they had to wait for America to be affected by at least 3-5 years of economic decline and the devaluation of the dollar. All of the problems America had been involved in, both domestically and internationally, had to weaken the government. Vigilance and military programs had been cut to the bone. Everyone was worried about the economy and stupidly ignored everything else, when one day they woke up too late to an EMP pulse bomb detonation. There were simultaneous land invasions from the south in Mexico and the sea along both coasts in North Carolina and Southern California.

Without electricity, the United States was in chaos and could not coordinate any response to repel the initial attack. Most of the country did not realize we were under attack. After a few weeks, the battle lines had been drawn and we were fighting in a World War I/Civil War-type battle.

The pigeons were brought to the front lines and messages were sent to various command posts about troop movements, wins, losses as well as other crucial war plans. The horse and wagon was the largest grouping of land transportation. The U.S. Postal Service was horse and bicycle driven. 1 out of every 5 people carried mail by foot. Vintage WWI & WWII cannons were taken out of moth balls for the battles.

The enemy advancement was halted at the edge of North Carolina on the Eastern Front and Alabama on the Southern Front. Half of California was overrun before they were stopped by valiant Army and civilian units. The battle lines were drawn and everything seemed to be at a standstill.

Since there was no school, Austin was sent to the Virginia Military base on the eastern coast of Virginia to watch over the pigeon coop #1.

The birds had been sent ahead 2 weeks earlier. They were Walter, the two champs, Lucy and her two friends and seven other birds. When he arrived there, Walter and four of the birds were on a mission, and when he went to the General's quarters to check in, he saw Mumford. After some fanfare, he finds out Mumford doesn't even know Walter's there.

At the base, the General and his aides were going over war strategies with other military brass. Mumford was perched on the top of his large cage whose door was always open. He went in-and-out at will. The officers were very loud with their opinions and observations. A young soldier reported to the desk of the General and stood at rapt attention. "Yes, Private?," the General mumbled through the stub of his unlit cigar.

"An important message has just arrived from the Eastern Front, Sir."

"Bring the bird in, Son."

CHAPTER 7

Discovering a Spy

The soldier left the room only to return moments later with a pigeon. [Possibly for a brief comedic effect the bird could be wearing a helmet reminiscent of the old WWI helmets many wore in France, i.e. The flat-rimmed, bowl-topped helmets.] Placing the pigeon on the desktop, the Private returned to attention as the General opened his desk drawer and retrieved a tool designed to remove the message tags. The General instructed the soldier to hold the bird while he removed the message.

"Walter?! Is that you?!," Mumford cried as he flew over to the General's desk. Walter cooed excitedly as the General and soldier watched in amazement.

"So, Mumford, you know this little guy?"

Mumford flapped and squealed excitedly.

"Ok, everybody," the General began, "out. Assembly is at 0500 hours tomorrow. Sleep tight, Gentlemen."

Everyone hustled out of the room except for the General's closest aide, Sergeant Kaiser. The two men then turned their attention to Mumford.

"Well?," the General did not need to say more.

"This is my friend Walter from Kearny, New Jersey, where you bought me."

"You mean he's from the pigeon coop there?"

"Yes, Sir! Walter's the best pigeon and he's very smart, too."

Turning his attention to Walter, Walter snapped to attention and offered a crisp salute.

"Hello, Son," the General said, returning the salute. "Thank you for your valuable service to this country."

The General then opened the message that came from the Eastern Front and read it to himself before turning to Kaiser and explaining that the front lines needed reinforcements as well as food and supplies. The General told Kaiser to send a message back to the front that they'd have their needed troops and supplies in two days. "And Sergeant, bring in some food and water for Walter. He'll be going out with the troops in the morning."

The General locked several maps in his desk drawer as Kaiser returned with the food and water, turned off all the lights except his desktop lamp and bid 'good-night' to the two birds before following Kaiser out of the office.

The two birds spent the rest of the night talking and catching up on what they had been going through. How Mumford had been kidnapped and then sold to the General, how Walter had gone through training and then the war came and since has seen a lot of action. Fighting, bombs, and a lot of dying people as well as his bird friends.

"How do you know where they want you to fly?" Mumford asked.

"Well, I'll always fly back to the last place I've been as long as I spend a few days there. They can take me pretty far away from that location, but as soon as I take to the air I just know which direction to fly. I think my Maker just made me that way. It's a knowing I know nothing about. When we're at a particular coop, we fly around the area several times a day. This gets us familiar with the area and it stays in our minds so at the end of our journey we know we have arrived."

Mumford was awestruck. "Wow, you pigeons are awesome. How many missions have you flown?"

"Awe, I don't count Mumford, but lots and lots. The enemy tries to shoot us down, ya know. My unit is down eight pigeons, we started with 13. Four initially never came back. Since I have flown a few close-calls myself, I can guess what happened to them. Bad weather, attacks by other animals and gunfire, of course. Those are the things that get us the most. Where you choose to rest along the way can be your most dangerous time in the whole journey. Well, Mumford, we've talked a long time tonight. We need sleep. Good night, my friend."

"Good night, Walter." Mumford fell fast asleep, still in awe of his friend.

The next morning, a small convoy of wagons headed out for the Eastern Front consisting of about 100 soldiers, five wagonloads of supplies and three pigeons in a large wooden cage. One was Walter, the other two were also from the Kearny coop, Barny and Hilda, two of the nicer birds in the bunch. Most of the upper echelon birds were very jealous of Walter's meteoric rise and status in the coop. His unusual thinking patterns had kept him alive on missions where all others never returned. But Barny and Hilda were always friendly towards him.

The next day, as the convoy was nearing it's destination on a bumpy back road, all hell broke loose. There was the familiar sound of gunfire and explosions. They were being ambushed! Every wagon was being riddled with bullets and the soldiers in the convoy were being cut down by the hidden murderers before they even realized what was happening. Just then a stray round sailed through the wagon flying through the cage, instantly killing Walter's two friends. Walter was briefly knocked down and stunned by flying debris from the hole in the cage as the bullet passed. Regaining is senses, he shot out the hole in the side of the cage and landed on some boxes. All suddenly became quiet, much too quiet. Then Walter heard voices approaching, but the men were speaking in a language different from those of the officers and people he knew. He could not understand what the voices were saying. "Uh oh," he thought to himself, "we're in enemy hands." Then he heard the door at the back of the wagon being unlocked and he readied himself. As soon as the doors swung opened, he shot out into the open air above the men's heads before they had any hope of reacting. As he screeched by, he took notice of the troops and confirmed to himself that they were in fact the enemy army. They're uniforms were different and they had different skin tones than the humans he knew. But one of the new humans seemed familiar to him. He was the one who opened the wagon door. The red scarf around his neck as well as his manner seemed *very* familiar. His voice also had a familiar ring to it as Walter heard him shout, "Shoot the bird! Shoot the bird! Don't just stand there looking, we must kill all their birds!!"

Bullets whizzed by Walter's head, but he was already too far away to be hit. The adrenaline rushing through his body took some time to wear off. But he flew on and on, mile after mile until he realized he didn't have to fly at such a breakneck speed. He lowered his altitude and glided for some time thinking of his two friends that were killed in an instant, right before his eyes. "How did things get so crazy so fast?," he wondered to himself. He used to live an uneventful life back in Kearny, New Jersey with his family. And now, this craziness. But a large part of him did love the excitement and challenge of this purpose-driven life. He would never go back even though he missed his family very much. They had no idea what he was into.

Walter was nearing the compound where the General and Mumford were waiting for his return, just not *this* soon.

There it was, the military compound. The smell of horses and cooking smoke in the air then sight of the familiar rooftops and his coop, where Sgt Vega and a few other pigeons were fast asleep.

Walter landed on top of the coop with a loud THUMP, waking the pigeons up.

"Walter," quizzed Sgt Vega, "is that you? What the hell are you doing here?" Vega blew a whistle and soon two Privates came rushing across the roof to the coop. They grabbed Walter and were off in a flash to the General's barracks.

Moments later, the knocking on his door jarred him out of a deep sleep. Opening the door, the Private carrying Walter said, "sorry to bother you, General, but we have one of the birds that left with the Eastern Front's convoy yesterday."

"Come in!," he told the men. Turning toward his desk said, "Mumford, get up! Your little friend is back. Only too soon!"

The soldier placed Walter on the General's desk as Mumford flew over and landed next to his friend. "Walter, what the heck happened, dude?"

"Oh, Mumford, they're all dead! The enemy attacked us. I got away when they opened the back of the wagon. But, Mumford, one of the enemy humans seemed familiar, as if I've seen or heard him before!"

"Maybe that's how they knew your convoy was on the way to the battlefront. I think we might have a spy or traitor in our midst!," the parrot said excitedly.

The two birds circled each other, flapping their wings and cooing and cackling at a rapid pace. The General watched them for some minutes then said, "What's going on, Mumford? Why is Walter back so soon with no messages?"

Mumford turned to the General and explained in detail what Walter conveyed to him. "Walter is the only survivor, Sir."

"What?!," growled the General, as his cigar dropped to the desktop. "All gone? Is he sure?"

"Yes, General, but there is more. But I can only tell you in private."

The General understood his meaning and dismissed all the other soldiers in the room. The three were suddenly alone in the quiet, darkened room. "Go on, Mumford."

"Walter believes there is a spy in our ranks."

"Spy?! Who?"

"He's not sure, Sir, but he said the person seemed and sounded very familiar, though in all the excitement, he may have imagined it."

"No, this all adds up. Some of the problems we have been having in the past are beginning to make more sense. Walter, we've got to get you back to the front. And we'll have to go by a completely different route."

The next morning, Walter was headed back toward the Eastern Front with more than 2,000 soldiers and a large convoy of supplies. He was now being guarded by two Rangers in a secret, heavily-armored wagon unknown to anyone else except the General. Walter had become irreplaceable. Walter was also instructed to keep vigilant as to the possible identity of the traitor.

Eddie missed his friend Walter very much. They had never been separated from each other since early childhood and Walter was usually the 'take charge' bird, but now Eddie was the lead bird and it actually felt quite good. Eddie distinguished himself in the field of service; he had a keen intuition of when to fly high or low or rest or seek refuge in a small or large town. He seemed to know if there was any danger from local predators. Out of 13 birds, 3 remained alive. When a message couldn't get through and there were missing birds and all hope was lost, they would send Eddie with a desperate message attached, and he made it every time.

When Eddie heard the first gunshot or felt bullets whizzing by he would fly in an erratic pattern to minimize his chances of being hit; no other bird but Walter would go into such maneuvers. The messages he carried would help the American effort in their attempt to defeat the enemy, assisted the plans of their hopeful victory come to fruition and, like his friend Walter, he was much revered and honored. He was very much looking forward to seeing his best friend and brother as the war came to it's conclusion.

Two months had passed and the days were getting shorter as the cool nights and the fall season were setting in. The enemy was planning a counter-offensive, but it all hinged on the Americans not being able to successfully communicate. So the enemy employed a number of exceptional sharpshooters at various points around the countryside. If any carrier pigeon flew overhead, the shooters had orders to shoot to kill on sight, thus preventing any messages getting through to either the central command post or the mobile command posts along the front lines. The sharpshooters were all in place and well-ingrained into the countryside.

The Americans noticed a lot of activity and movement on the enemy side. So they correctly assumed something big was in the works. The top brass along the Eastern Front decided to send a warning message to the central command informing them of the enemy troop movements. Walter had made four trips the previous two months, so they opted to send one of their champion pigeons, Cal, to home base. Walter and Cal were talking about the mission, kidding each other about who was better, but all the kidding aside, they had enormous respect for each other.

Two men came to the coop to take Cal and release him for the mission. Walter noticed that one of the Privates was a new soldier. That something seemed familiar about him. When the soldier spoke, Walter was immediately assaulted with the realization that the man was the same one that was at the ambushed convoy! He was the Spy! He took Cal and held him while the other soldier tied the message to his feet. The Spy let Cal go and Cal took off sharply on his mission.

The one soldier was very friendly, always talking to the pigeons and Walter especially. There were 7 pigeons left in the coop. The other man looked dark, ominous and threatening, never smiling at all and always seemed preoccupied in thought.

"We must go now, Tom," the Dark One said.

"Ok, Sir," he replied, "but I love these guys. They're doing such a great job, especially Walter here. He's the luckiest bird of the whole launch."

"Yes . . . I know," he replied slowly, "but you know what they say, *luck will someday run out,*" and he closed the door.

Cal was flying at a good pace above the countryside. "Just another flight," he thought to himself. "I don't have to rush."

On a hilltop, up ahead of Cal, an enemy sharpshooter was scanning the horizon with his binoculars, watching for birds. "Ah," he said softly, "a pigeon. Come to papa." He raised his rifle and took aim at the unaware bird. "A little closer, my friend," then pulled the trigger. The bird exploded in mid-air, and what little pieces there were, fell to the ground.

Back at the base, the General paced back and forth by his opened window. "Mumford, one of your buddies is long overdue, unless they didn't send him."

As part of their routine, the birds were sent out at the same time each day they were needed for a mission.

"I think we'll send a bird out with a question mark to see what the problem is."

A young female pigeon was chosen and sent to the Eastern Front with her message. The General took no chances.

"We can't afford to wait until morning. If they sent a bird out this morning, he's long overdue."

Hours later, the female, named Lucy, fluttered down on top of the coop at the mobile command post. She was lucky. The sky was darkening and the enemy was not looking for birds coming from the north in the evenings. Most, if not all, of their attention was turned toward the southern daylight-lit skies to stop requests from the battlefronts. The six remaining birds in Walter's unit were resting and were startled when Lucy landed on top of their coop.

"Lucy! What's going on, girl?," Walter asked. "How's Cal?"

"I didn't see Cal, was he sent?"

"Yeah, this morning," he replied.

Her heart sank at the realization that they may never see Cal again. "Oh my, he never showed up. Maybe he's hurt or something, maybe lost."

Walter went cold and he fluffed his feathers nervously. "This is not good and I think I know why."

One of the soldiers on guard quickly ran to the coop and swooped Lucy up and hustled her away.

The mobile base's Colonel stood rigidly some moments later, looking at the message that contained only a question mark. "Oh no, our bird didn't make it through." He looked toward the soldier and said, "Quickly, get two more birds, no, three. At least one of those birds must get through to the command center. We need reinforcements and supplies if we're to hold this line."

Three soldiers returned to the coop and quickly grabbed three pigeons, two of which were Walter and the other champion bird, Joab. It was dawn and the sun was just beginning to brighten the sky.

Each bird was outfitted with an identical cryptic message requesting men and supplies and alerting the central command that three birds were sent. The birds were off and up in a flash.

At first, the three flew in their usual tight formation, but it occurred to Walter that they were too easy a target to hit. "Look, Joab," he called to the remaining champ, "we have to fly farther apart. They are trying to shoot us down. Let's make their job as hard as possible."

"Sounds like a good plan," Joab replied.

Walter counted to three and the birds beautifully separated apart so nearly 100 feet were between them and they soared six- to seven- hundred feet off the ground and on they flew to the north.

Sometime later, one of the sharpshooters was casually looking at the scenery to the south when he noticed a bird off to his left. He did a double- and triple- take when he caught the movement of the other two birds in his field of vision. "Can't be pigeons," he thought to himself, "they only fly in tight formations." Taking a closer look he exclaimed aloud "they are pigeons!," and dropped the binoculars and grabbed his rifle as the birds were nearly upon him. The bird to his right was shakily in his sights. He had no time to miss, as there were three targets this time. He squeezed the trigger and the bird exploded soundlessly. The shooter quickly moved his gun to the left, hastily fired and missed. He fired again and again, but missed the two birds as they flew overhead, veered off and dropped in altitude. He reset his stance and fired rapidly at the center bird. "Got you!," he shouted as he hit the bird in the wing, causing the bird to spiral down in circles to the ground. Wasting no time, he fired quick shots at the third and final bird, and the bullets whizzed by Walter as if he was standing still. He must do something or he was going to end up like his two dear friends. He dropped straight down like he did in the first race against the two champions. As he dropped, he could hear the gun fire three more times, but Walter was not there anymore. He leveled off just above the trees and continued to fly low, which made him an impossible target. "Oh, God," he thought to himself. He could not believe his two friends were gone.

He flew on and on in desperation, without resting, until the familiar rooftops of the Army base came into view. Walter landed on top of the coop, startling the other pigeons. A guard came and retrieved Walter and carried him immediately to the General.

The General read the coded message and told Kaiser to immediately mobilize the base. "Mumford, talk to Walter and find out what's really going on," he said.

After warmly greeting each other, Walter explained in great detail what had been happening at the mobile base and on his flight north. Mumford flew over onto the General's desk and said, "General, Walter said that there are sharpshooters stationed in between the fly points to stop the birds from getting to their destinations. He was sent out with two other birds, but they were shot down trying to reach us. And he said that he saw one of the enemy soldiers that ambushed the convoy. He was at the mobile post, posing as one of our soldiers just before Walter was released on his mission."

The General was so angry that he bit his cigar in two. "The spy, huh? We're gonna take care of him, to be sure. Thank you, Walter," he said, saluting him.

A siren went off in the evening air and the whole fort was abuzz as a beehive.

CHAPTER 8

Help From Below

Horses had become a large part of American life and Army life. They were recruited from everywhere possible; all farms, horse stables and race tracks were nationalized and drawn from. Carpenters all over the U.S. were building horse wagons large and small to be used to move troops, equipment and food to wherever needed. Horses and carrier pigeons were in great demand. Pigeon coops were exploding on the scene all across the country to satisfy the demand for more pigeons. Last but not least, the salvageable coal-driven locomotives were brought out of moth balls and put to work for cross-country travel, military and civilian.

Horses and wagons began pouring into the military base in great numbers, lining up by the barracks. The soldiers poured into the wagons by the hundreds and thousands. The General came over to the two birds and cleared his throat. "Hmm, ok, boys, chat time is over. Walter has to go back to the front with the convoy tonight." Sgt Kaiser gently grabbed Walter and carried him through the door. They hid Walter somewhere in the middle of the convoy for his safety, for he had become the "Go-To" bird. Soon they were off into the night. Seven-thousand troops, ammunition, supplies, food, guns, and Walter, the link between the front and home base. Walter hated these rides; they were too noisy, bumpy, smelly and anything but restful and they seemed to last forever. Walter heard the familiar sound of cannon fire in the distance, so he knew his journey was almost complete.

Soon he was back in the large coop in the mobile command post talking to his friends. He told them what had happened to Joab and the other bird that was sent with them; they were stunned beyond belief.

Both Champions were gone, things would never be the same and everyone was sad for days. During the many openings of the cage by the different soldiers, Walter noticed one night that the cage door had been left ajar. Walter flew over to the door and pushed it wide open, "Wow, this is great! I've wanted to get out and look around for someone. This must be the will of the Maker." And out he flew, gliding back and forth over the busy compound, his eyes searching for the PX, the large building where the troops went to relax and have some downtime. He perched on the branch of a tree across from the front entrance and watched and waited as the soldiers came and went with much fanfare and camaraderie. He waited for a long, long time and was almost falling asleep when a lone figure with a red scarf and hat pulled down, looking cautiously from side to side, came through the door. He quickly walked off to his barracks.

"Oh, yeah," Walter thought to himself, "I knew I'd find you. Now I'm gonna find out what you're up to." He flew and glided soundlessly behind the soldier.

The soldier turned into the dark barracks and Walter circled until a light went on in the rear corner of the building. He flew over and perched on the ledge of the window; it was opened and Walter watched as two men stood over a table looking at a blueprint discussing plans.

'Red Scarf' was speaking: "The General's quarters are over here and the PX is here," one said pointing to the blueprint. "We'll put one device here, three in the PX and five in the large officers barracks. We must get this General now, or we'll lose this war. His battle strategy is brilliant and he must die. His command structure needs to be eliminated as well, those officers are key to the American's victory."

The other soldier shook his head, "Yes, Ahyube, we must turn this situation around or things will be over for us."

The red-scarved Ahyube rolled up the blueprints and said calmly, "Death to the American's, my friend. We cannot fail. Let's go."

"Oh, no!," Walter thought. He flew back to the coop and he talked to all the other pigeons, explaining everything that he'd discovered and telling them there was no time to lose. He told them he had to warn the General back at home base and was off at sunrise after a meal and a drink. He was hoping to pass through the cordon of shooters unnoticed as he was flying earlier than expected. But he was wrong. As the war was going very badly for them, they had increased their vigilance.

Walter flew through the early morning air; he knew he should keep low to the treetops, but would have trouble finding his destination at such a low altitude. So this early in the flight, he was forced to fly higher. "Maybe," he thought, "that it's too early for the shooters to be awake."

But one very young shooter was up very early as he had fallen asleep early the previous night. He was about to have himself some coffee when he saw a speck in the southeast sky that made him drop his coffee cup and run for his rifle. A lone pigeon, too early and too high, he noticed. He raised his sights and pulled the trigger twice in quick succession; the gun resounded.

Walter never heard the bullets until one whizzed by his head, but could not react in time as the second grazed his rear side, sending him into a tail spin. Then he heard more shots ring off and he instinctively dropped into his now-famous dive to avoid more gunfire. The boy whistled for his dog to retrieve the bird and off it went. Walter leveled off and perched in a tree checking out his wound. No flying feathers were hit; though the wound just burned and bled a bit. Suddenly the dog burst on the scene darting this way and that, very confused. There was no dead bird on the ground. After some time, he went back to his trainer.

Walter sat on the branch shivering from shock. He was checking out his wound when he heard a small voice. "Psst, psst, over here, pal." Walter looked over to see a squirrel in the next tree waving his paws. "What's a pigeon doing out here, dude?"

"Oh, hi," replied Walter, "I'm flying a mission, for the people of the land we live in, we're at war, ya know." Walter went on to explain the whole mess to the squirrel whose mouth remained open in amazement.

"Wow, dude, we have to help you get your message to your friends up north," he said. He introduced himself as Augie.

"How can you help me get out of here, Augie?"

"No problem, I got connections out here, they call me 'The Mayor'. I know everyone and everyone knows me. We all look out for each other out here."

"I don't know how I'm going to get past the shooters."

"Me either, but first things first, let's talk to the sparrows."

"Sparrows?," Walter asked.

"Yeah, the sparrows, they're everywhere and are usually very helpful with wise advice," Augie explained.

Augie ran down his tree and started running down the path. "Let's go, Walter! No time to waste!"

Walter glided behind Augie and they traveled about a mile to a clearing. Augie climbed onto a large elevated rock and motioned for Walter to join him.

"What now?," Walter asked.

"Shush. Just wait."

After just a few minutes, one by one, the sparrows came asking questions but never stopped their erratic activity. Walter again explained the whole story to these hyper little creatures.

"I have an idea who can help you," said Marnie, the leader. "The starlings are your only hope," she said solemnly. "We must find them before they leave!"

"Where are they going?," asked the squirrel.

"The migration, it will start soon!," she said incredulously. "Let's go!"

Walter, Augie, Marnie and friends traveled through the woods about 5 miles to a large clearing that as they approached it became louder and louder. The field was huge and covered in black from start to finish, millions of starlings milling about waiting for takeoff orders. The starlings seemed to barely notice the small band of intruders. Marnie shouted as loud as she could for someone important to talk to. Finally two starlings listened to her rants and asked what she wanted. These birds were tough, scrappy birds, even the huge black birds were no match for them in the sky or on the ground and there were just too many of them.

Marnie told them it was an emergency and she needed to talk to the boss.

"Easier said than done," said Rocky, the larger of the two birds.

"Look, I don't care how hard it is, your whole way of life and safety depends on us speaking to your leader!," she implored.

"Ok, ok. Worm boy," he said to the other bird, "get Uncle Floyd now."

The smaller bird disappeared into the flock immediately.

About 10 minutes went by and the black sea parted and Worm Boy led 6 or 7 very important looking starlings to the edge of the crowd to meet with Walter and his troop.

"Why do you bother me at a time like this, little Marnie? You know the time is near," said the impressive-looking Floyd.

Marnie looked to Walter and introduced them. They both told Floyd the story one more time and waited for his reaction. "Well, we know there is something strange going on in this land. Loud noises and death. Fire has been seen south of here, so what you're saying makes sense. Walter, we'll help you to get north to your General and friends. Although I can't understand any bird getting close to any human period. They smell bad and are violent. We'll fly cover for you and fly north until you are safe, then start our migration. Is this acceptable?"

"Floyd, Sir, I can't thank you enough."

"Well, son, let's go."

That night they camped with the starlings and had a lot of fun together and fell asleep bunched together. The next morning, they all said their "good-bye's" and Walter stood alone before the starling nation.

"Ok, Son," Floyd barked, "You leave first and set your altitude and we'll leave a minute later, but we fly faster so we'll catch up to you."

Walter was off like a shot and when he reached the correct altitude he leveled off; he sensed he was getting near the shooters zone, so he started to fly erratic patterns until the starlings came up behind. Walter was spotted by at least three shooters with their long-range binoculars. "Here comes one! Not in range yet, but he's flying erratically, so sharpen your aim, boys." They all picked up their rifles and took aim. "Not in range yet, come on pigie, just a little closer . . . a little closer. You're about there, ok . . . ok. What the hell?!-"

Suddenly, the lone silhouette of the pigeon was blocked by the sky becoming black behind it. The men lowered their rifles and stared in amazement. The formerly sun-filled clear sky was blotted in black by millions of starlings flying behind Walter. The men looked at each other and shrugged their shoulders. "I hope that pigeon doesn't have any important messages. There's no way to shoot it down now." The man said in resignation, "what luck."

"You'd better hope it was luck and not providence, my friend, or we're all in big trouble," explained the other soldier.

The starlings were everywhere in the sky and Walter was in the middle of the large pack. They slowed down to his steady pace and flew with him for about a half-hour. Then Floyd flew next to him and shouted, "Ok, Son, you're on your own. I think you're safe now."

"Thank you, Sir," yelled Walter. "You guys are the best, may the Maker bless you all."

"Yes, He does and He will continue to. May He be the lifter of your wings. Goodbye and good flight, Walter."

Floyd whistled and the whole flock dropped right out of the sky to a large meadow below and to the left. Walter watched them momentarily then proceeded to the military base.

CHAPTER 9

Final flight

A few hours later, Walter landed on top of the coop in the barracks. There were only three birds left in the cage, his girlfriend, Lucy, and two other birds.

"Walter!," cried Lucy, "what's up? You don't have a message on your leg."

"No, Lucy," he explained, "I've come on my own to warn the General of a terrible danger." The two soldiers on guard came over to check on Walter. One picked him up and observed that he had no tag. "Something's up, dude, there's no tag. Maybe he just got loose. I'll put him back in the cage until the General gets out of his meeting."

'Oh, no!,' thought Walter, 'staying in this cage won't do at all. I must get to the General.'

They quickly put Walter back in the cage and ran off. The General came back to his office, greeted by Mumford. He was tired and sat down heavily at his desk, resting his face on his fingers. "Hello, Mumford. How are you, boy?"

"Hi, General. How are you, Sir?"

"Doing quite good, boy. We're getting ready to throw these bums out of our country."

There was a knock at the door.

"Come in," the General said and the two soldiers came through the door. "Any news from the front?"

"No, Sir, but the bird Walter landed about an hour ago with no message," one soldier answered.

"No message?," queried the General. Looking at Mumford he asked, "What do you think, Mumf?"

"Not good, Sir, can I talk to him, please?"

"Yes, you must talk to him, he didn't fly up here for nothing." Turning toward the soldiers he said, "Get him!"

Minutes later, Walter was being placed on the General's desk. Walter and Mumford exchanged their usual excited greetings, cackling and cooing round and round in a circle. Then both looked at the General and Mumford spoke. "General, you're in grave danger. A spy with a red scarf will or has already placed a bomb here and in the main barracks."

What?! Who? How the hell-," the General began, but Mumford cut him off. "Walter has been watching this guy for some time, he masterminded the ambush last month and Walter heard him making plans with other spies."

Well, I'll be," said the General. Looking around nervously, thinking there could already be a bomb in his quarters. His eyes fell on the two soldiers, "Private, run to the main barracks and evacuate it immediately. Do the same for the officer's barracks."

The two grunts saluted quickly and were off in a flash.

Moments later there was another knock at the door.

"Yes," queried the General.

"Cleaning detail, Sir," replied a voice.

The General walked over and opened the door. "You guys aren't due for two more days. Where's Private Haryton?"

"He's sick, Sir. We were told to come today."

"Hmph. Ok, I'll go have dinner."

The men hurried past the General carrying the cleaning supplies, or so it would seem. The General fumbled around at his desk, talking to Mumford, "Ok, boys, I'm going to get some chow. I'll be back in half an hour."

But one of the soldiers kept looking over at Walter very nervously. The man looked familiar thought Walter, 'no red scarf, but this guy could be the spy guy.'

Just then a siren went off outside the barracks. It meant that the barracks were being evacuated. Walter told Mumford about the two cleaners and Mumford flew over to the General's shoulder.

"What's up, boy?," he startled.

But before he could speak the spy wheeled around pointing a pistol directly at the General. "Hands up, General. Sounds as if our plans have been discovered, so I'll have to take matters into my own hands."

Walter looked intently at the spy; he hated this human. This man killed many of his friends and now he was going to kill the General and Mumford. In a flash, Walter shot across the room, hitting the gun hand of the spy. The gun went off and dropped to the floor. The General reached for his pistol and aimed at the two men, shooting both of them in the legs. The door to the General's office burst open and two MP's came in, rifles ready.

"Get these two spies out of here to the Infirmary, then for questioning. Are you ok, Walter? You are something else, bird. You are a Special Forces bird, if there ever was one." The General then ran into the bathroom and came out, white-faced. "There's a bomb in the latrine, boys! Let's get out of here fast, it could go off at any moment!"

He grabbed both birds and ran out of the building. Outside, hundreds of men were running everywhere, men streaming out of the PX and the officers leaving their quarters. "Get the Bomb Squad to each of these buildings," he shouted.

But no sooner than the words left his mouth when they went off. First the General's quarters, then the officer's then the PX. Thank God the men were out of the buildings. Thank God and this little pigeon named Walter. Everyone hit the ground then got to the business of fighting the fires.

The Next day, through the clearing smoke, the General and his officers planned the final counter-attack. To once and for all throw these invaders out of his country. In three days they would travel southwest to position themselves west of the enemy in a coordinated attack; catch the enemy off-guard and defeat them. The current line of defense would create a diversionary attack and then the General's forces would surprise attack them from the rear side.

So 5 coded messages were sent via the last 5 birds. Word was sent north that the bomb blast was successful and many big wigs were killed. The enemy would be thinking they were close to victory just before their big defeat.

The General stood before the 5 birds and spoke to Walter. "Walter, I'm asking you just one more time to bring these messages to our friends in NC. At least one of you must get through. Everything depends on it."

Every half hour they let one pigeon go, but Walter asked Mumford to let him and Lucy go at the same time; he just had a feeling about it, and of course, they did whatever Walter asked.

Walter and Lucy were nearing the danger zone. Halfway out, Walter insisted they stop to rest so he could talk to her about their future if they made it. "Lucy, what do you think about having children," he asked.

"Children? Now? With all this going on?," she puzzled.

"No," he countered, "I mean when this is all over and we're back in Kearny."

"Oh," she replied. "Sure I want little ones, are you asking me to be your mate?"

Walter panicked. "Uh, well, I mean-yes, you know I care for you."

"And I adore you, Walter, but let's get through this thing first, ok?"

"Ok, Lucy," Walter said as they nestled close together for a while and then took off to finish their mission.

The shooters knew something was up when three birds were sent at half-hour intervals. Each one meeting it's demise, so they scanned the northern sky to see if there were any more coming. It was almost sundown when they saw Walter and Lucy in their binoculars. "Oh, here comes two," shouted one man and they raised their rifles and got off two rounds. One whizzed past Walter's head and then struck Lucy in the wingtip. She went into a spiral dive and Walter jumped on her falling body, causing it to go into a straight dive. The shooters couldn't get off any finishing shots, so they sent the dogs. When they hit the ground, Walter dragged her behind a tree. She was in shock. He then waited for the dogs. Within seconds they were on the scene. Walter's plan was to have the dogs chase him away from her and into the woods.

He feigned injury. Scratching the ground, scratching and flapping his wings, the two dogs were on him in seconds. He quickly darted over their heads in the opposite direction and landed, faking injury again. They swallowed it, hook, line and sinker. Contrary to popular opinion, dogs were stupid, thought Walter. Especially hunting dogs; he despised them. It was actually fun leading these two dolts farther and farther away from Lucy.

Augie heard the shots, the dogs and the commotion caused by the Walter, so he came down from one of his favorite trees to the edge of the clearing and he heard soft moaning and cooing behind a maple tree. Oh, God, it was a girl pigeon and she was shot through the wing. She was just coming out of shock. He then whistled in a very high-pitch tone for his friends. In virtually seconds, five squirrels came to the clearing edge from different directions, "What's up, Augie?," one asked.

He pointed toward the struggling pigeon, "She needs our help, she's been shot. Get a stretcher now."

Two of them split off into the woods immediately. Less than a minute later they were back with a large lily pad. They gently rolled the injured Lucy onto the pad and were about to leave when Walter fluttered down right next to them.

"Augie!," he cried. "What are you doing?"

"Hey, Walter, why am I not surprised to see you in all this mayhem? We're getting this girl some help," he explained.

"Thanks, Augie, you're the best. She's my girl, ya know. Can you take care of her til I get back? My mission is not finished. Everything depends on my message getting through."

"Sure, Walter. We'll take good care of her. You know where to find us, right?," he asked.

"Yeah."

Walter went over to Lucy and spoke softly to her as she looked up at him intently.

"These are my friends, Lucy," he explained. "You're going to be down for a few weeks and I will come back for you, so you just relax and get better. I must go, I must get through."

With tears in her eyes, she spoke to Walter, "That's why I love you, you have destiny in your wings. I'll wait for you."

The silence was shattered by the sound of dogs barking.

"Uh oh," said Augie, "they're coming back."

"Ok, guys, beat it, I'll lead them away again."

The squirrels were off in a flash through the woods and Walter waited for the dogs. They came into the clearing and spotted him immediately.

"Ok, boys, let's have some fun," and he was off in the other direction with the dogs screeching at his heels. He flew low at a breakneck speed right over the shooter's station. They saw him momentarily but could not get a shot off. "Well, we got one, but this one will never make it back past us coming north again, so I think we're ok."

Walter stayed real close to the treetops for about 10 miles, then he regained proper altitude and about an hour later he landed on the coop at the front. The soldiers brought him right to the commander and promptly read the coded message. "This is it guys, game over in three days, prepare for attack."

CHAPTER 10

Victory

One day later, under a heavy cloud of secrecy, the strike force left Virginia along with the General and Mumford, some 3,000 troops and munitions, thousands of carts pulled by horses. This was it, the one-two punch and a knockout one at that. The General had been waiting for this day for some time.

Two days later the activity was frantic in Walter's camp. They were getting ready to attack on the third day. Walter mused at all the commotion around him, but his thoughts were on Lucy and what she was going through. He longed to be with her, but now it was time to fight the dastardly enemy and expel him from their land. He also couldn't wait to see Mumford and the General again and if he saw them, he would know that the people of his land were successful and the war would be over.

The next day, the attack began and the noise was deafening. The battle raged for about 4 hours until soldiers came for the birds. "Let's move these birds," a soldier shouted. "Things are going so well, the brass wants these birds moved closer to the action." So they loaded them into a cart and they were off. They were getting closer to the battle because Walter heard the guns getting louder and louder. For some time the noise was at an even keel, but then all hell broke loose and there were explosions all around them. "It's a counter-attack, boys!," shouted one of the officers. "Move the birds back, we must retreat!"

"Uh, oh," thought Walter, "we're now losing? Will I ever see my Lucy again?"

Bullets whizzed by everywhere. He saw soldiers who were going south now running north. Some were shot down all around him. His horse was struggling in the mud to make any headway. Things were rapidly deteriorating all around him. Then an artillery round hit their cart and it splintered into nothing.

Their cage tumbled over and over and came resting on it's side with the door wide open. The four pigeons scrambled out of the cage and flew to the top side of another cart that was upended in the race backwards. Things looked bad.

"Walter, what should we do?," asked one of the birds. "Should we fly back to base?"

"Not yet," said Walter, his eyes straining over the horizon.

"What are we waiting for, Walter? The enemy will be coming over that hill in minutes," he said pleadingly.

"For Mumford," he said with a pained look on his face. "He should be coming from the west right about now."

Suddenly from the west came a flurry of large explosions, a far trumpet sound and the sound of thousands of horses hooves. Bullets from the west filled the air. The incoming fire upon Walter and the Americans abruptly stopped. The 'two" portion of the one-two punch was in play; the enemy had no answer for what was upon them, they had expended all their energy pushing north and were completely outflanked and surprised. They never knew what hit them.

Like a wave, the American Western Front swallowed up the enemy who dropped their weapons by the thousands and gave up in surrender. And there he was in all his glory on a large Clydesdale horse, pistol in hand and cigar in his mouth with a colorful, strange little bird on his shoulder clinging for dear life. The General rode on, barking orders to the left and to the right, but all Walter was looking for was his little friend. Mumford made it! Who would have ever believed that this war in the East hinged upon the relationship between these two feathered friends and the information shared between them; above and beyond what they were called to do.

Mumford then spotted Walter and his friends. He yelled excitedly into the General's ear, "It's Walter! It's Walter, Sir, over there!"

The General stopped his horse and looked through the carnage only to see these 4 little pigeons sitting on top of an overturned cart. "Well, I'll be, there is a God in Heaven that cares about pigeons!" The horse strode over to the cart. Mumford flew off the General's shoulder and landed almost on top of Walter; the two danced around and around, cooed and cackled and rubbed up against each other.

"We did it, buddy!" cried Mumford, "but were you getting nervous?"

"A little," said Walter. "But I knew you guys were coming."

"Yeah," said Mumford, "that was the plan the General and I cooked up two weeks ago. I'm so glad he listened to me!" They both laughed loudly.

The war was over within weeks. The enemy was defeated in the south and California soon afterwards. Walter's best friend Eddie distinguished himself in the service on the Southern Front and was reunited with Walter within days. Electricity was making a quick comeback. Limited truck and auto movement began again.

Back at the North Carolina front, grandstands and bleachers were set up for the big celebration. Jets and helicopters ringed the skies. The people took to their seats, the soldiers stood at attention in ranks of the thousands, dignitaries stood on the top platform and the military bands played. Confetti flowed in the air like a snowstorm. It was magnificent.

On the main stage stood the President of the United sates and many Senatorial dignitaries, the three top Generals and many Colonels, but at the end of the platform was a mid-sized cage with Walter, Eddie and two other heroes of the Western front. The speeches went on one after another and Medals of Honor and Purple Hearts were given out to the brave soldiers who earned them.

"Taps" was played for the lost warriors and they all cried. But last and not least the General stepped to the podium to a round of applause, for he was well-loved and respected. All became quiet and he cleared his throat. "My fellow Americans, we have weathered the most egregious of storms ever to hit this beloved land. Never since we have become a nation have we been so close to extinction. But the American Spirit would not capitulate to the dastardly machinations of this ruthless enemy. This test has brought out the best in the American Spirit during the worst of times. But my friends, we would not be here today it if weren't for these small creatures who sit patiently at the end of this stage. When all modern-day communications were lost, we were forced to use an ancient method of sending and receiving messages only known to the military. During this process, it was discovered that we had a ring of spies. One extraordinary bird named Walter told my little friend Mumford here who they were and it saved the lives of many, many soldiers; people including myself.

"So, my friends, we honor 4 extraordinary birds whom God placed at the right time and the right place; who represent hundreds of their brothers today." He motioned for the cage to be brought forth. "My fellow Americans, I give you the real heroes!" The place went berserk with pandemonium and elation.

But wait, there were only two birds in the cage, Walter and Eddie were gone. The General and Mumford looked nervously around and the crowd became quiet. Walter and Eddie were circling the review stand, cooing to Mumford.

"Where are they going, Mumford?," the General asked.

"Walter's going to find Lucy. She's recovering in the forest in North Carolina."

The General smiled and saluted the two departing birds.

"My fellow Americans, Walter and Eddie have been sent on a very important secret mission. Let's give them a hand!" The place went nuts! The boys smiled down at the pandemonium and shot off in a northerly direction.

About two hours later they were approaching the sniper's zone.

"Are we close, Walter?," Eddie cried.

"Yep. Normally I'd be nervous about the shooters, but now I'm nervous about seeing Lucy again. I hope she's better by now."

Eddie flew closer to Walter, "Oh, sure, man. She's tough and smart and pretty, too! Don't you worry, Walter."

Walter smiled. "Yeah, she is pretty, huh? I think she's a knockout."

A short time later, Walter recognized the countryside. "Oh, there's the field, let's go down, he barked.

The two birds swooped down on one large log in the field and looked around intently. Coo! Coo! Walter cried again and again. After a few minutes there stood a familiar figure on the other end of the log. "Well, it's about time, Walt boy. What took you so long? Who's your friend?," quizzed Augie.

"Augie!," Walter cried. Then a serious look formed on his face. "Where's Lucy? Oh, I'm sorry, this is my friend, Eddie."

"Hey, Eddie," said Augie. "Are you another hero like Walter?," he quizzed.

"Yeah, you might say that, Augie. Everybody else does." Then he laughed.

"Well, Augie?!," Walter cried.

"Oh, I'm sorry, Walter," he said apologetically. "Your girlfriend is fine. All she does is talk about you and we all have one big question. Did you guys win this war?"

Walter paused and smiled, "We sure did, Augie. We kicked their asses good!"

"Whew," sighed Augie. "We were worried for you all. Let's go to the camp."

The three friends went through the forest and arrived at the starling clearing.

This time of the year the field was normally deserted and quiet, but as soon as the three friends broke into the open, the place went wild with a million starling bird cheers. The field was full of birds, but there were all sorts of birds, robins, wrens, bluebirds, black birds and other animals were present. Raccoons, badgers, wolves, chipmunks and all varieties of forest creatures. But today, they were all friends.

Walter and Eddie were blown away by this celebration. The commotion lasted for many, many minutes and then died down when Floyd came through the crowd. Behind him followed the entire Pigeon family from Kearny; Walter's Mom and Dad, brothers and sisters and all his friends. "Welcome home, lads," said King Floyd motioning toward his family. The boys were overrun by their families, emotions running high; they hadn't seen the boys for six months!

There were high-fives and hugging and snuggling up to each other. Walter then asked King Floyd, "How are you guys back here and how did you get my family here?"

"We had to come back to celebrate and Lucy arranged to have your family here," he retorted.

"Lucy!," he cried. "Where is she?," he demanded.

"Why, she's right behind you, dummy!," he responded.

Walter wheeled around quickly to see the most beautiful sight. Lucy, with a beautiful white band around her head and streamers flowing down her body, she had tears in her eyes and love on her face and in her heart. They opened their wings and held each other for a long time.

Floyd tapped Walter on the shoulder, "Hmm, hmm, young man, your attention, please." The King then turned to the noisy throng and raised his wings. "My fellow animals and birds, may I have your attention, please!," he shouted. All became quiet.

"For as long as I can remember, pigeons were the least respected and most maligned of all the bird family. Not foragers, not gatherers, not hunters, but beggars and loafers. They had all but forgotten their storied past. But now we realize that these birds are blessed with guts and talents that catapult them to the head of the bird family. And now we honor them today and thank especially these three pigeons who went above and beyond the call of duty to this beloved land of ours. So, Walter, Lucy and Eddie, we honor you today as our great heroes." He motioned with his wings and all the creatures bowed down low to the ground leaving these three little birds looking nervously around and over the great crowd.

"Oh, my good friends," yelled Walter. "We couldn't have done this without your help, and for that we will be eternally grateful to you all. Maybe this is a beginning of us not being so separated as tribes or family different from each other. But we can't forget all the other pigeons who lost their lives. So on their behalf, I accept your devotion. Can we have a minute of silence for them?"

After a moment of silence, Eddie lifted his wings and said, "Get up, dudes! Let's party!"

And they did, all afternoon and evening, long on into a brand new day.